At the Pond

Written by
Stephen Rickard

I went
to the pond.

At the pond,
I saw a frog.

I saw a small,
brown frog.

At the pond,
I saw a dragonfly.

I saw a red dragonfly.

At the pond,
I saw ducks.

One duck,
two ducks,
three ducks.

At the pond,
I saw flowers.

I saw big, pink flowers.

At the pond,
I saw fish too.